THE
RED SPORTS CAR

All inquiries should be addressed to:
Barron's Educational Series, Inc.
250 Wireless Boulevard
Hauppauge, New York 11788

Library of Congress Catalog Card No. 87-35937
International Standard Book No. 0-8120-3937-8

Library of Congress Cataloging-in-Publication Data
Sklenitzka, Franz Sales.
  [Rote Sportwagen. English]
  The red sports car / Franz S. Sklenitzka : translated from the
German by Elizabeth D. Crawford.
    p.   cm.
  Translation of: Rote Sportwagen.
  Summary: The hare and the hedgehog buy a flashy fast car and take
it for a spin, but they are dismayed to find out how impractical it
is for them.
  ISBN 0-8120-3937-8
  [1. Hares—Fiction. 2. Hedgehogs—Fiction. 3. Automobiles—
Fiction.] 1. Title.
PZ7.S62833Re 1988
[E]—dc19   87-35937
                                                        CIP
                                                         AC

PRINTED IN THE UNITED STATES OF AMERICA
890 9770 987654321

BARRON'S ARCH BOOKS SERIES

Franz S. Sklenitzka

THE
RED SPORTS CAR

With Illustrations by the Author

Translated from the German
by Elizabeth D. Crawford

BARRON'S

New York • London • Toronto • Sydney

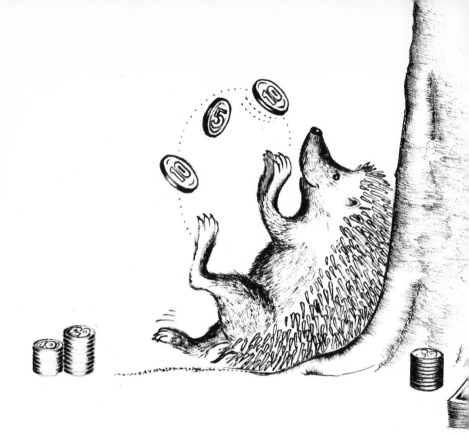

The hare and the hedgehog

had a pile of money,

more money

than they could count.

They had gotten the money
from a race Hare had run
against Tortoise for
television.

Now the two friends
sat in the field
and thought about
what to do.

"We could buy
something to eat,"
the hare said.
All that thinking
had made him hungry.

"We could do that,"

the hedgehog agreed.

"But I was thinking

of something more practical!"

"Eating *is* practical!"

said the hare.

"Corn on the cob is practical.

Carrots are practical.

Beets are practical."

"I was thinking about a car,"

said Hedgehog.

"Holy cabbage patch!"
cried the hare.
"A car?
You can't eat that!"
"Of course not,"
said the hedgehog.
"But with a car
you can go very fast—
even faster than a fox!"

"Even faster

than a weasel?"

asked the hare.

"Sure!" said the hedgehog.

"Faster than a dog?"

asked the hare.

"Sure!" said the hedgehog.

"And with a car

you can drive from

one feeding place to the next!"

That made sense to the hare.

"From the beet field to
the cabbage patch!"
he cried happily.
"From chicken coop
to chicken coop,"
said the hedgehog.
He just loved eggs.
"Hedgehog, you always
have the best ideas!"
said Hare.
"Come on—let's go buy a car!"

So the two friends

went to a car dealer.

"What'll it be?"

asked the salesman.

"A car," said the hedgehog.

"A fast car!" said the hare.

"Yes, it should be fast—

as fast as a hedgehog!"

said the hedgehog.

"As quick as a hare!"

said the hare quickly.

"Faster than a fox!"
the hedgehog declared.
"Faster than a weasel!"
said the hare.
"Faster than a hound dog!"
they both said together.
The car salesman laughed.
"There are," he said,

"cars that are faster

than the fastest animals."

"We'd like a car like that,"

said Hare and Hedgehog.

"Fast cars are not cheap,"

said the car salesman.

"Do you have any money?"

"And how! More money

than you can count!"

cried the hedgehog.

"Which car is the fastest?"

The salesman pointed to
a red sports car.

"Good, we'll take it!"
said Hare and Hedgehog.

So they bought

the red sports car.

That wonderful car

had a convertible roof.

If it rained,

you could pull up the roof

like an umbrella.

If the sun was shining,

you could fold it back down.

"Holy cabbage patch!"
sighed the hare.
"What a wonderful car!
I could just cry with joy!"
"Go right ahead!"
said the hedgehog.
So the hare cried a little.
Then he dried his tears
with his ears.
For of course he had
no handkerchief.

And then they drove away.

The hedgehog sat
behind the steering wheel.
First they drove
on a track through the fields.

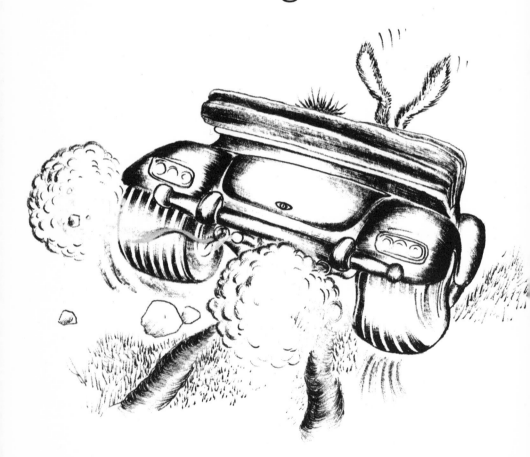

There were lots of stones

in the field.

The red sports car

bumped and thumped,

so they could

only go very slowly.

Then they tried a country road.

But there were too many curves

on the country road,

so they couldn't drive

very fast there, either.

When they saw a farmer,
the hedgehog
slammed on the brakes.
"People aren't stupid," he said.
"And farmers usually know
a thing or two!
Oh, farmer!
Where can you try out
a fast car around here?"
The farmer looked at
the red car.

He scratched
behind his ear.
He had never seen
a hare and a hedgehog
in a car before.
Then the farmer said,
"You can drive fast
on the freeway.
Take your first left,
then left again,
and then left again."

"Thanks!"
called Hare and Hedgehog.
And off
they drove.

On the
freeway
the cars went whizzing past
into the distance.
Most of the cars
were driven by people.

Terrified,

the hare and the hedgehog

sat at the side of the freeway

in their red sports car.

Terrified,

they looked at each other.

"Why are the people

driving so fast?"

asked the hedgehog.

"They don't have anything

to be afraid of!"

"No fox is chasing them!"

"No weasel!"

"No hound dog!"

"No eagle!"

"No one is following them,
and yet they are rushing along
as if something terrible
were after them,"
said the hedgehog.

"Don't you understand?"
cried the hare.

"It's a race!

We've run a race ourselves!

This is an automobile race!"

That made sense to Hedgehog.

"They don't just race

two at a time in this one,"

cried the hare.

"There are many more!

Let me drive!"

That was all right

with the hedgehog.

The hare was bigger
than the hedgehog
and could see the road better.
The hare seated himself
behind the steering wheel.
The hedgehog moved over
to the passenger seat.
"Step on the gas, Hare!"
cried the hedgehog.
"Maybe we can still win!"
The hare stepped on the gas.

Faster and faster

the red sports car flew along.

The hare's ears

flapped

and snapped

in the wind.

First they passed
a yellow car.
Then a blue one.
Then another blue one,
and a dark red one,
and a brown one.
"We're doing it!
We're doing it!"
cried the hedgehog.
He clapped his front paws
with excitement.

"Come on, Hare!" he screamed.

"There are only

three more cars ahead of us!"

The hare drove even faster.

He passed the three cars.

Now they could no longer see

one single car ahead of them

on the freeway.

"Hurrah!" shouted Hedgehog.

"We're in the lead!

We're way out in front!"

The hare drove still faster.

His long ears

whirled in the wind

like a propeller.

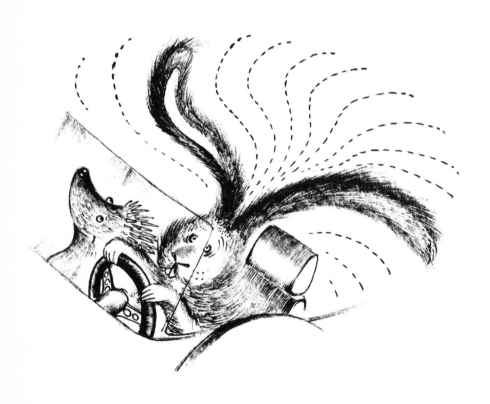

Suddenly,

in the far distance,

a tiny green dot appeared.

"What's that?" cried the hare.

"Get closer to it!"

cried the hedgehog.

"We'll soon see!"

So the hare drove

still faster.

The tiny green dot

soon became a bigger green dot.

The bigger green dot
became a green truck.
"We've got to pass that!"
cried the hedgehog.
The red sports car
whizzed past
the green truck.
"Now we're
in first place again,"
said the hare happily.

He rejoiced
a little too soon.
In the far distance,
there where the freeway
was as thin
as a hair from a fox's beard,
a tiny little point
appeared again.
This time it was white.
"What's that?" cried the hare.

"Get closer to it!"

the hedgehog shouted.

"We'll soon see!"

The hare drove even faster.

His long ears

streamed out

longer and longer.

Soon the tiny white dot

turned into a bigger white dot.

The bigger white dot

turned into a white van.

"There's one we still

have to pass!"

cried the hedgehog.

The red sports car

dashed past

the white van.

Now the freeway
lay empty before them again.
"We are in first place!"
Exclaimed the hare gleefully.
Joyfully he drummed
on the steering wheel
with his front feet.
"Holy cabbage patch!
I could just sing for joy!"
"Go right ahead!"
said the hedgehog.

The hare sang.

He sang, "All my hares run
even faster than the sun."

Then he sang, "The hare is
such a lovely beast,
why does Fox choose him
for a feast?"

Suddenly
the hare
stopped singing.

He had heard
someone cough.
"Have you caught
a cold, Hedgehog?
Shall I
put the top up?"
"Why?" asked the hedgehog.
"Because you coughed,"
answered the hare.
"I? I didn't cough!"
said the hedgehog.

"I thought you coughed!"

said the hedgehog.

"But I didn't!"

cried the hare in amazement.

"The car!" cried the hedgehog.

"The engine coughed!"

It really did.

The engine coughed.

It coughed again.

All at once it stopped

purring smoothly.

The sports car
rolled more and more slowly
until it finally came to a stop.
"What's wrong?"
cried Hare and Hedgehog
at the same time.
They jumped out of the car
and walked around it,
looking carefully on all sides.
"It doesn't look sick,"
said the hare.

"They sell you a car,"
the hedgehog complained,
"and after ten minutes
of driving, it stops!"
Helplessly,
the hare and the hedgehog
walked around the red car.

Meanwhile,
the white van
drove by.
Soon it was only
a tiny white dot
in the distance.
The green truck
rolled past.
Soon it too
could barely be seen
in the distance.

Three more cars drove past.

Then came a brown car.

Behind it was a dark red one.

Two blue cars

whizzed by.

"Mean!"

the hedgehog scolded.

"People don't stop to help!"

"Not one of those pigs

even slowed down,"

complained the hare.

All the cars and trucks

they had passed before

went right on past them.

Then came a yellow car.

The yellow car drove slowly.

It stopped beside the red

hare-hedgehog-sports car.

A badger climbed out

of the yellow car.

"What's wrong?" asked the

badger in a friendly voice.

"If we only knew!"

sighed the hare.

"No idea!"

sighed the hedgehog.

"Do you have enough gas?"

asked the friendly badger.

"Why?" asked the hedgehog.

"To drive a car

you have to have gas,

of course, you wise guys,"

said the badger, laughing.

"If the engine

doesn't get anything to drink,

it doesn't run.

May I?"

The badger

looked at the gas gauge.

"Yes, there we have it!"

he said.

"Not a drop of gas in the tank!"

"What now?"

asked Hare and Hedgehog.

The friendly badger

went to his yellow car.

He took a can

out of the trunk.

He carried the can over to

the red sports car

and emptied a little gas

into the tank of

the hare-hedgehog car.

"I'm sorry I don't have any

more," said the badger.

"But it will get you
to the next gas station
where you can tank up."
"We could call it a *tank stop*,"
said the hedgehog.
"Then I could say *tanks* a lot!"
The badger laughed.
"You really are
out of it, aren't you?"
Hare and Hedgehog didn't
want to be out of anything.

"We are in the middle of it!"

said the hedgehog.

"We are way out

in front of it!" cried the hare.

"Aha," rumbled the badger.

"That's what I thought.

That's exactly what I thought.

In any case, drive to

the next gas station now.

Have your car filled up there.

Then you can drive on."

"Aha," said the hare.
"We'd like
to thank you,"
said the hedgehog.
"Even if this isn't
a *thanks stop*."
"Yes, many thanks,"
said the hare.
"Glad to do it!"
cried the badger.

"Don't forget
to look at your
gas gauge

from time to time!"
Then the badger climbed
into his yellow car
and drove off.
"Now we're the last again!"
wailed the hare.
He was close to tears.

"I could just cry
at our bad luck!" he moaned.
"Go right ahead!"
said the hedgehog.
The hare cried a little.
Then he dried his tears
with his ears.
He had no handkerchief,
of course.

"Isn't it sad

when you are last?"

wailed the hare.

"But it hasn't happened yet,"

the hedgehog comforted him.

"The others have to stop

and fill up somewhere, too.

Then we'll pass them again.

We'll pass them all again!"

"Do you think so?"

asked the hare.

After a short drive
they came
to a gas station.
Beside the gas pump
stood a rat.
The rat had a cap
on his head.
"Hello!"
said the rat
"I'm the attendant."

"Hello!"

said Hare and Hedgehog.

"We have no more gas

in the tank."

"I could have guessed,"

said the rat.

"But gas isn't cheap!

Gas costs money!

Can you

pay for it?"

"And how!" said the hedgehog.

"We have more money
than you can count!"
"Now, now Hedgehog,
don't say that!
It isn't so much money
anymore."

The red sports car
had a big tank.
The big tank guzzled
a lot of gas.

The hare and the hedgehog
had to pay a lot.
"Can we get something
to eat here, too?"
asked the hare.
He had noticed a restaurant
next to the gas station.
"If you can pay,"
said the rat.
"We have it all here.
Everything your heart desires."

"And how we can pay!"
said the hare.
"You've already seen
that we can pay!
We have more money than
you can count!"
The hedgehog said nothing
They really didn't have
that much money anymore.
The hare climbed out
of the red sports car.

Driving had

made him hungry.

The hedgehog stayed

in the car.

The hare

ordered ten carrots

from the waitress.

And a head of cabbage.

And a small bag of clover.

And a green salad.

Without mayonnaise.

"To go or
to eat here?"
asked the waitress.

"The carrots
and the cabbage
to go,"
said the hare.
"The clover and the salad
to eat here.
But no mayonnaise
on anything!"

When the hedgehog saw
that the hare
had ordered a lot to eat,
he got hungry, too.
He climbed out of the car
and ordered twenty snails
and a soft-boiled egg.
"With mayonnaise?"
asked the waitress.
"Without,"
answered the hedgehog.

"The snails

without mayonnaise, too!"

"Will that be to go

or to eat here?"

asked the waitress.

"The soft-boiled egg

to eat here!

The snails can come with me."

"The snails

can come with us?"

cried the hare.

"They can't
keep up with us.
They're much slower
than our sports car!"
"You're off your rocker!"
cried the hedgehog.
"The snails
are going
in the trunk!"
"No way!" cried the hare.
"Those snails

will eat my carrots
and my cabbage!"
"I'll pack the snails
in a jar for you,"
said the waitress.
"Thanks," said the hare.
"Very nice of you,"
said the hedgehog.

Then the hare ate the clover
and the green salad.
The hedgehog ate his
soft-boiled egg.
The hare packed the carrots
and the cabbage
into the trunk.
The hedgehog packed the jar
with the snails
into the trunk.
They tried to close it.

But the trunk
wouldn't close.
As hard as the hare
and the hedgehog
pressed down on the lid,
it popped right up again.
"Too much in there!"
said the hedgehog.
"Yes," said the hare.
"You should eat
some of the things."

"Do you think so?"

asked the hedgehog.

He took a snail

out of the jar

and ate it.

"Maybe that will do it,"

he said.

But the lid

still wouldn't close.

The hedgehog took another snail

out of the jar.

He ate that one, too.

But the trunk lid

still could not

be closed.

"I can't eat any more!"

panted the hedgehog.

"Now it's your turn!"

The hare took a carrot

out of the trunk

and crunched it down.

Then he crunched a second one,
and a third.

"Maybe it will close now,"
he said.

Yes!

At last the lid could be closed.

"Funny!" said the hare.

"When you eat a snail,
it doesn't do anything.

But if I eat carrots,
there's more room in the trunk!"

"Uff," groaned the hedgehog.

"I am really very full!"

The hare stroked

the hedgehog's

tummy

with his hare's foot.

"Round as a ball!"

he said.

"I'm much too full, too.

See—

feel my tummy!"

The hedgehog stroked
the hare's tummy
with his hedgehog's foot.
"Round as a ball!" he said.
"You won't need any
supper tonight."
"Neither will you,"
said the hare.
With difficulty,
they squeezed themselves
into the red sports car.

There was hardly any room
for the little round hare-tummy
behind the steering wheel.
"Uff!" groaned the hedgehog.
"You should buy cars
on full stomachs,
not on empty ones!"
"You're right there,"
groaned the hare.
"Now we have to get going!
We still want to win!"

He started the car
and drove it
from the gas station
back onto the freeway.
Soon the sports car
was flying along
at top speed again.
The hare's ears flapped
and snapped. They whirled
like a propeller, and
spun out longer and longer.

The red sports car passed
one car after another.
Suddenly
the hedgehog struck
his forehead
with his front paw.
"Hare!" he screamed. "Hare!
We're going
in the wrong direction!
We're going back
where we came from!"

"Are you sure?"

asked the hare, horrified.

"Very sure!"

cried the hedgehog.

"Just now we passed a big,

bare tree."

"Yes, and . . . ?" asked Hare.

"I saw the same tree

before we got

to the gas station!"

cried the hedgehog.

"We're going back
where we came from!"
"Holy cabbage patch!"
wailed the hare.
He was close to tears.
"I feel like crying,"
he said with a sigh.
"Go right ahead!"
said the hedgehog.
Then the hare cried a bit,
but he didn't drive any slower.

Then he dried

his tears

with his ears.

That's right!

He still had

no handkerchief with him,

of course.

"Isn't that sad?"

he wailed.

"First,

the gas runs out on us.

And now we are driving
in the wrong direction!
Hedgehog, I'm afraid
we're not going to win!"
"We are!" said the hedgehog.
"How come?" asked the hare.
"Because the other drivers
don't know
where the finish is."
"How come?" asked the hare.
"Do we know?"

"Sure," said the hedgehog.

"We know. At least I know."

"Tell me, too!"

begged the hare.

"The finish,"

declared the hedgehog,

"is at the car dealer's!"

"How come?" asked the hare.

"The race goes from

the car dealer's

to the gas station.

And back to the car dealer's
again," declared the hedgehog.
"That was the start
and that's the finish.
But we're the only ones
who know that."
"Then we can still win!"
cried the hare happily.
"Sure," said the hedgehog.
"Who else?"
The hare was silent.

After a while he asked,
"And what shall we do
at the finish?"
"We'll give the car
back to the dealer,"
said the hedgehog.
The hare nodded.
"And the dealer will give us
back the money."
The hedgehog nodded.
"Agreed!" said the hare.

"Done!" said the hedgehog.
"The sports car
isn't as practical
as you thought, is it?"
asked the hare.
"No," answered the hedgehog.
"That it is not."

After a short time
they got off
the freeway.

Soon they found their way to

the car dealer's showroom.

The car salesman

was astonished

when he saw them both again.

"What will it be this time?"

he asked.

"Another car for the gentleman

with the cactus haircut?"

"No, thank you!"

said the hedgehog.

"We don't need
a second car,"
said the hare.
"We don't even need
one car,"
said the hedgehog.
"We don't need
a car at all!"
"Why are you coming
to see me
at all, then?"

The car salesman
was annoyed.
"We want
to give back
the red sports car,"
replied the hedgehog.
"It's not practical!"
said the hare.
"It's impractical!"
said the hedgehog.
"Why?" asked the salesman.

"Isn't it fast enough?"

"Yes. But it is

too thirsty!" declared the hare.

"It needs too much gas."

"Yes," said the hedgehog.

"The tank is too big."

"Yes," said the hare,

"and the trunk is too small."

"Yes," said the hedgehog,

"and the seats

are too narrow."

"That's especially true
if you've eaten a big meal,"
added the hare.
"Very well,"
said the salesman.
"I'll take back
the red sports car.
But I can't give you
as much money
as you paid
for the new car!"

"Why not?"

asked the hare.

"Because the car

isn't new anymore!"

declared the salesman.

"Aha," said the hare.

"That's all right with us,"

said the hedgehog.

"Perhaps you should buy

yourselves a van,"

suggested the salesman.

"Some other time, maybe!"
said the hedgehog.
He removed
the jar of snails
from the trunk.
"Yes, maybe some
other time!"
said the hare.
And he took the cabbage
and the carrots
out of the trunk.

Do you know how many
were left?
How many carrots?
And how many snails?
"Just enough for a nice snack,"
Hedgehog exclaimed.
Hare agreed.
So they walked off
together,
munching happily.

Other Barron's Arch Books that you will enjoy reading:

Ben and the Child of the Forest
Caroline Moves In